Get the Nest, Nelly!

W9-ATB-858

Written by Nancy Monson

Illustrated by Sarah Peterson

Get Out of the Nest, Nelly! Second Edition
ISBN: 978-0-9853549-0-9
Copyright©2012 by Author Nancy Monson
and Illustrator Sarah Peterson

Requests for information should be addressed to
Get Out of the Nest, LLC, PO Box 234, Lanesboro, MN 55949
Email: nancydee@yahoo.com or sarah@petersoncreative.net
Phone: 507-272-7859

More about Nelly online at www.getoutofthenest.com.

All rights reserved. No part of this publication may be reproduced,
stored in a retrieval system, or transmitted in any form or by any
means—electronic, mechanical, photocopy, recording, or any
other—except for brief quotations in printed reviews, without the
prior written permission of Nancy Monson and Sarah Peterson. This is
a work of fiction. Names, characters, places and incidents either are
products of the author's imagination or are used fictitiously. Any
resemblance to actual events or locales or persons, living or dead, is
entirely coincidental.

Layout and Design by Sarah Peterson

Five
baby
ducks — hatched
and were getting ready
to leave the nest…

Well, everybody but **Nelly** that is.

Nelly always found an excuse to stay behind.

"BUT I CAN'T!"
said Nelly.

"Don't you see that this wing
isn't long enough?

I will surely fall!"

Off flew her sisters
Deena,

Frannie,

& Freeda

and her brother Dexter.

Whenever they came back to visit
they would try to coax
her to leave, too.

"Get outta* the nest!"

"Come on Nelly!"

"You can do it!!!"

"It is SO much fun out here!"

As usual . . .

* slang for out of

One day her brother Dexter stopped and told Nelly about all the bugs and places he'd visited.

"I saw a cricket at Times Square

and a beetle
at the
Statue of Liberty.

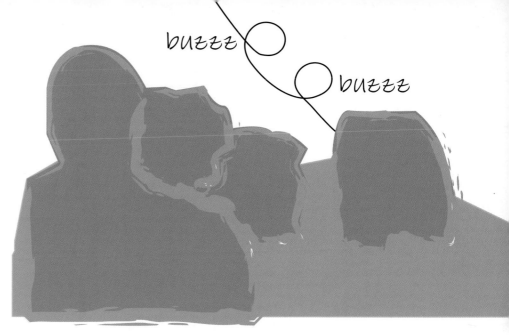

buzzz

buzzz

I'm hoping to see some
mosquitos at Mt. Rushmore.

Would you like to come along?
Who knows, we might even run into

an itsy bitsy spider...

or a very hungry caterpillar."

As usual...

Nelly said,

"BUT I CAN'T!"
"Who would stay and
clean up the nest
if I'm not here
to take care of it?"

Dexter flew off.

Next came her sister Deena. "Nelly, you need to come out and try some GREAT new foods!"

"I met a Bohemian Waxwing who ate over **600** berries in a single day!

That's TWICE its own body weight!!!

My favorite berry is the chokecherry
but I don't think I could eat 600 of them in one day!
Could you?

Come fly with me, Nelly."

As usual. . .

Nelly said,

"BUT I CAN'T!"

"What if I get tired from flying around all day?

I better stay here in my comfortable nest."

Another sister, Frannie,
returned and told Nelly
about her new friends.

"I have met penguins from Antarctica,

road runners from Arizona,

puffins
from Alaska,

and a ring-necked pheasant
from South Dakota.

Now I'm heading up to northern Minnesota to meet some loons!

Would you like to come along?"
As usual. . .

Nelly said,
"BUT I CAN'T!"

"I think I
need glasses.

All I can see
are the twigs in
my nest."

5 Great Lakes,

Superior

Huron

Michigan

Erie

Ontario

streams,

puddles and ponds,

and numerous bird baths.

I especially like the bird baths.

You'd like the feeling of a bird bath, Nelly.
Your nest is SOOOOO dry.

I crouch in the water and flick my wings
to spread water over my body.

Then I SHAKE the water off
my wings and preen my feathers.

I'm looking
SOOOOO GOOD
when I step
out of a bird bath!"

"I've seen all kinds of trees-

blue spruce,

white oak,

paper birch,

sugar maple,

flowering dogwood,
crabapple,
and red mulberry.

There are warm climates
and cold climates which
produce different
kinds of trees.

In fact, I'll be migrating
to a warmer place soon.

Would you like to come along?

Maybe we'll see some wild grape vines
or cottonwood trees along the way."

And, as usual. . .

Nelly said,
"BUT I CAN'T!"

"The world is too big.
I might get lost
if I leave.

I like my warm,
cozy nest."

The truth of the
matter was that
Nelly was growing
and the nest was
becoming more and more
uncomfortable.

In fact, the nest seemed
to be getting
smaller...

and smaller...

and smaller.

Nelly was beginning to feel miserable and lonely.

The only friend she had was Tom, the short-eared owl, who occasionally stopped by to visit.

"Hi Tom."

"Hi Nelly."

"How are you, Tom?"

"I'm great Nelly.
I just got back from
a fantastic trip.

This world is **incredible,**
          don't you think?"

Well, Nelly didn't really
know what to think.
She had never left the nest,
so she hadn't seen the world.

"You know, Tom, I'm getting a little lonely up here by myself, but I'm just too scared to leave.

What if I'm not good enough?

What if I fly south instead of north?

What if I fall down?"

"What if?"

"What if??"

"WHAT IF???"

"Now, now Nelly...
no bird is expected to be perfect.
If you fall down,
you can pick yourself up.

If you find you're going the wrong way,
you can change your direction.

It's really quite simple."

"Just get out of the nest!"

Then Nelly said the unexpected.

She wiggled her wings, shook off the dust,
and with a hop and a skip
she launched herself into the air

- and she SOARED!

She saw crickets
and ants,

oceans
and lakes,

Superior

Huron

Ontario

Erie

Michigan

sunflower seeds
and raisins,

penguins
and puffins.

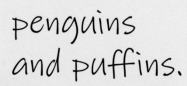

That was when Nelly finally began to enjoy
her new and wonderful, fun-filled life.

In a warmer place she found her brother and sisters.

And oh. . .
the stories
she had to share.

"I heard Nelly
wants to
fly to
Canada!"

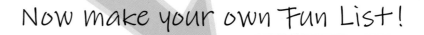
Now make your own Fun List!

Nelly's Fun List

- ☐ Visit friends in Canada
- ☐ Learn to play pickleball
- ☐ Take drum lessons
- ☐ Memorize state birds
- ☐ Bake cookies
- ☐ Plan a biking trip
- ☐ Take swimming lessons
- ☐ Find Big Dipper in the night sky

_____'s Fun List
(write your name here)

- ☐ _____
- ☐ _____
- ☐ _____
- ☐ _____
- ☐ _____
- ☐ _____

What's pickleball, Charlie???

I don't know, but it sure sounds like a lot of fun to me.